For Dad

First Edition, September 2017

10 9 8 7 6 5 4 3 2 1
FAC-029191-17167
Printed in Malaysia
Illustrations were created in silkscreen and digital collage

Library of Congress Cataloging-in-Publication Data

Names: Pizzoli, Greg, author.
Title: The twelve days of Christmas / Greg Pizzoli.
Other titles: Twelve days of Christmas (English folk song)
Description: First edition. Los Angeles ; New York : Disney Hyperion, 2017.
Summary: An elephant parent has to take responsibility for caring for all of the gifts
that arrive in this newly illustrated version of the traditional song.
Identifiers: LCCN 2016032327   ISBN 9781484750315 (hardcover)
ISBN 1484750314 (hardcover)
Subjects: LCSH: Folk songs, English—Texts. Christmas music—Texts
CYAC: Folk songs—England. Christmas music.
Classification: LCC PZ8.3.P558687 Twe 2017   DDC 782.42/1723 [E]—dc23
LC record available at https://lccn.loc.gov/2016032327

Reinforced binding

Visit www.DisneyBooks.com

THE 12 DAYS OF CHRISTMAS

GREG PIZZOLI

DISNEP · HYPERION ✳ Los Angeles ✳ New York

On the **FIRST** day of Christmas,
my true love gave to me . . .

A partridge in a pear tree.

On the **SECOND** day of Christmas,
my true love gave to me . . .

Two turtle doves,
And a partridge in a pear tree.

On the **THIRD** day of Christmas,
my true love gave to me . . .

Three French hens,
Two turtle doves,
And a partridge in a pear tree.

On the **FOURTH** day of Christmas,
my true love gave to me . . .

Four calling birds,
Three French hens,
Two turtle doves,
And a partridge in a pear tree.

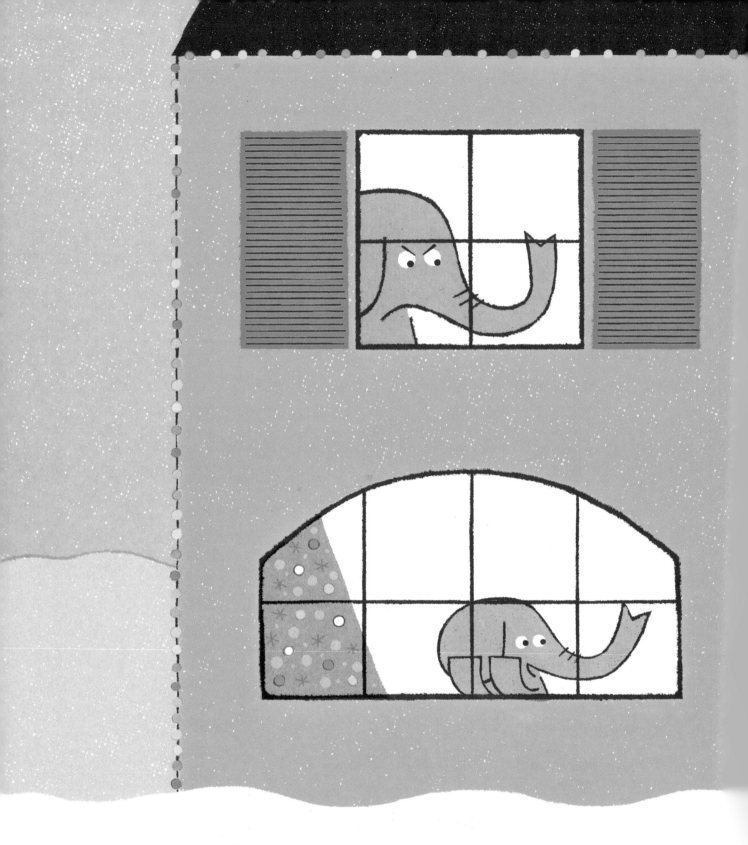

On the **FIFTH** day of Christmas,

my true love gave to me . . .

Five golden rings,

Four calling birds,
Three French hens,
Two turtle doves,
And a partridge in a pear tree.

PHEW!

BULK BIRDSEED

On the **SIXTH** day of Christmas,
my true love gave to me . . .

Six geese a-laying,

Five golden rings,

Four calling birds,

Three French hens,

Two turtle doves,

And a partridge in a pear tree.

On the **SEVENTH** day of Christmas,
my true love gave to me . . .

Seven swans a-swimming,

Six geese a-laying,

Five golden rings,

Four calling birds,

Three French hens,

Two turtle doves,

And a partridge in a pear tree.

On the **EIGHTH** day of Christmas,
my true love gave to me . . .

Eight maids a-milking,
Seven swans a-swimming,
Six geese a-laying,
Five golden rings,
Four calling birds,
Three French hens,
Two turtle doves,
And a partridge in a pear tree.

On the **NINTH** day of Christmas,
my true love gave to me . . .

Nine ladies dancing,
Eight maids a-milking,
Seven swans a-swimming,
Six geese a-laying,
Five golden rings,
Four calling birds,
Three French hens,
Two turtle doves,
And a partridge in a pear tree.

On the **TENTH** day of Christmas,
my true love gave to me . . .

Ten lords a-leaping,
Nine ladies dancing,
Eight maids a-milking,
Seven swans a-swimming,
Six geese a-laying,
Five golden rings,
Four calling birds,
Three French hens,
Two turtle doves,
And a partridge
in a pear tree.

On the **ELEVENTH** day of Christmas,
my true love gave to me . . .

Eleven pipers piping,
Ten lords a-leaping,
Nine ladies dancing,
Eight maids a-milking,
Seven swans a-swimming,
Six geese a-laying,
Five golden rings,
Four calling birds,
Three French hens,
Two turtle doves,
And a partridge in a pear tree.

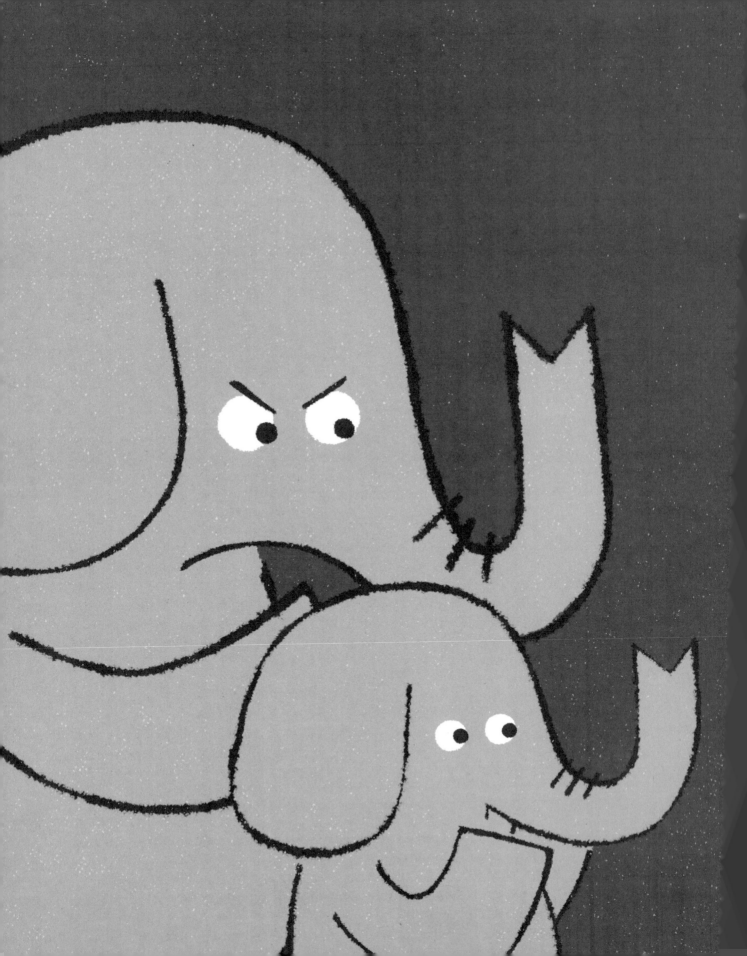

On the **TWELFTH** day of Christmas,
my true love gave to me . . .

12 DRUMMERS DRUMMING

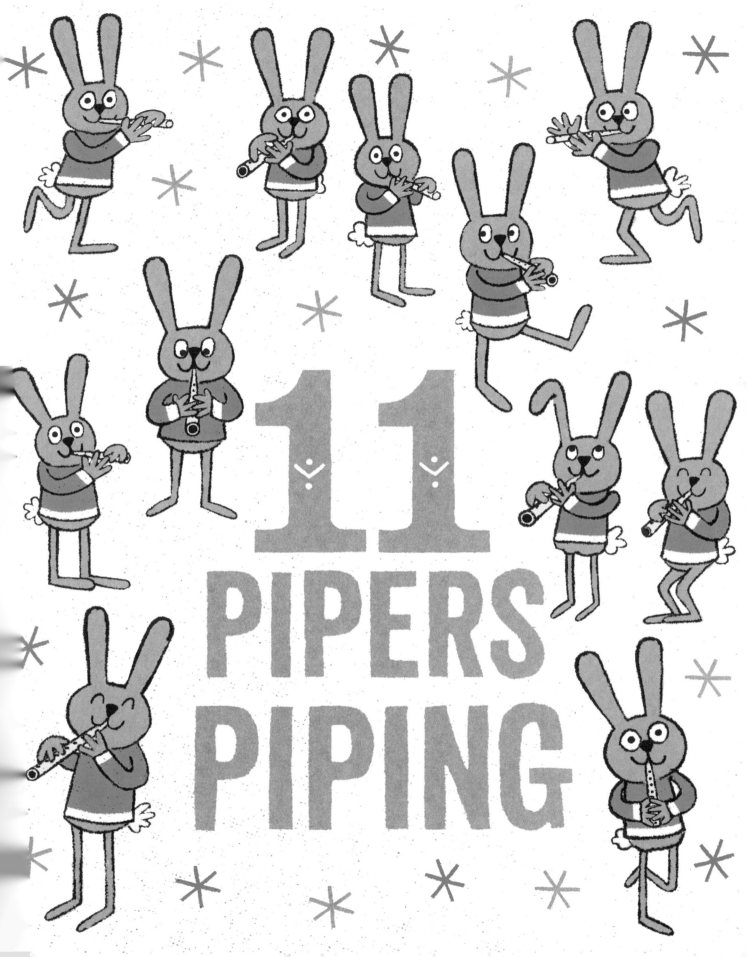

10 LORDS
A-LEAPING

7 SWANS
A-SWIMMING

6 GEESE A-LAYING

5 GOLDEN RINGS

And a partridge in a pear tree!